THIS BOOK BELONGS TO

This edition first published in the United Kingdom in 2012 by
Pavilion Children's Books
10 Southcombe Street
London, W14 0RA

An imprint of Anova Books Company Ltd

Design and layout © 2012 Pavilion
Text and Illustrations © 2012 Nicola L Robinson

ISBN 978-1-84365-200-7

A CIP catalogue record for this book is available from the British Library.

10 9 8 7 6 5 4 3 2 1

Reproduction by Dot Gradations Ltd, UK
Printed and bound by Toppan Leefung Printing Ltd, China.

This book can be ordered directly from the publisher online at
www.anovabooks.com

THE MONSTER MACHINE

Nicola L Robinson

My Dad is an inventor.

He spends all his time in his workshop inventing things...

He has just finished his latest and greatest invention.

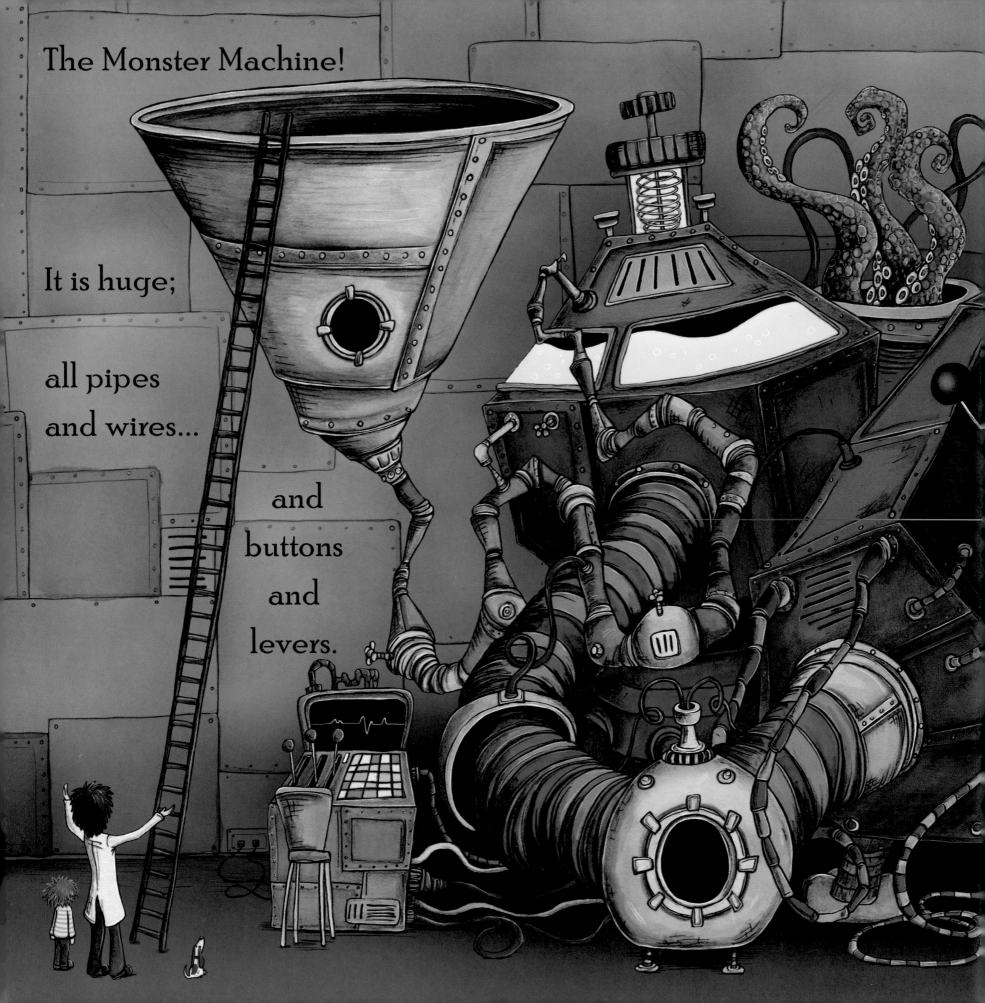

The Monster Machine!

It is huge;

all pipes
and wires...

and
buttons
and
levers.

It has a big funnel at the top where Dad puts all the ingredients to make the monsters.

Monsters are made of lots of things...

Slugs,

bogies,

toenail clippings,

sprouts,

earwax,

spiders,

and some

special dust

and goo

from

Dad's

cupboard.

We put all the ingredients into the machine.

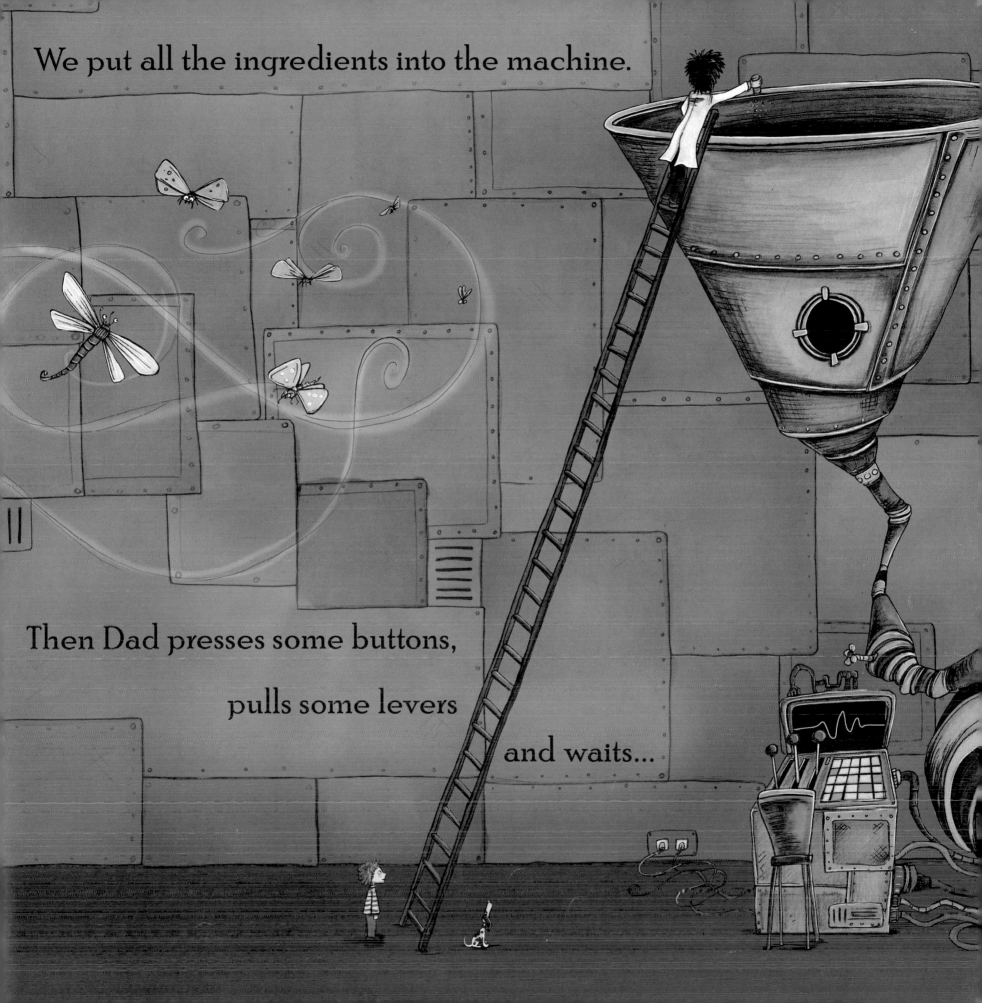

Then Dad presses some buttons,

pulls some levers

and waits...

The machine starts to rumble
and rattle,
and shake...

Smoke
and steam
spurt out...

Lights flash on
and off...

Then
something
falls
down
the
chute...

then another...

and another...

Monsters! The Monster Machine makes all kinds of monsters.

Big ones...

Funny ones...

Scary ones...

Scaly ones...

Hairy ones...

And everything in-between.

The monsters know all kinds of things.

They teach me monster games

and monster tricks

and we have lots of fun
playing together.

But one day...

The monsters don't want to play anymore.
They had been reading books
and watching TV,
and made a discovery.

Monsters don't belong in this world. Their home is far away...

and it looked incredible.

They wanted to go.

But how?

Dad has an idea to help,
which makes the monsters very excited...

They would build their own machine, a real monster machine...

and
chiselled

and sanded

and polished

and painted.

Soon it was
finished.

A flying machine!

It's huge

with giant wings...

and tall sails...

and wires
and buttons
and levers.

The monsters pack their
things and climb aboard
and start the propellers
ready for take off.

Bye bye monsters!

Now there's only one monster in the house...

And that's ME!